For

Emily, Sophie, Felix, and Ben

◇◇

THIS IS A BORZOI BOOK PUBLISHED BY ALFRED A. KNOPF, INC.

Copyright © 1985 by Helen Craig
All rights reserved under International and Pan-American Copyright
Conventions. Published in the United States by Alfred A. Knopf, Inc.,
New York. Distributed by Random House, Inc., New York.
Published in Great Britain by Walker Books, Ltd., London
First American Edition.
Manufactured in Vicenza, Italy. 10 9 8 7 6 5 4 3 2 1

Library of Congress Cataloging in Publication Data
Craig, Helen.
The night of the paper bag monsters.
Summary: Pig friends Susie and Alfred quarrel
while preparing for a costume party but make up in
time to go together as scary paper bag monsters.
1. Children's stories, English. [1. Pigs–Fiction.
2. Costume–Fiction. 3. Parties–Fiction] I. Title.
II. Title: Night of the paper bag monsters.
PZ7.C84418Su 1985 [E] 84-25045
ISBN 0-394-87307-6 ISBN 0-394-97307-0 (lib. bdg.)

SUSIE AND ALFRED

IN

THE NIGHT OF THE
PAPER BAG MONSTERS

HELEN CRAIG

ALFRED A. KNOPF · NEW YORK

Susie was spending the day with Alfred.
He was worried. "We must think of something
to wear to the Halloween party tonight," he said.
"Shall we go as ghosts?" suggested Susie.

"Whooo, whooo, whooo!" howled the ghosts.
"Hello, Susie! Hello, Alfred!
   Having fun?" said Alfred's mother.

"This is no good," complained Alfred. "We must do something so different that no one will recognize us."

In the garden shed they found
some very strong paper bags.

"Grrr, grrr, grrr!" growled Alfred. "I'm a terrible monster!"
"No, you're not," said Susie. "You're a pig in a
brown paper bag!"

"Let's paint faces on the bags then," said Alfred,
    and they set to work.

Everything was going very well until Alfred stepped
back to admire his work. He accidentally knocked
a can of green paint all over Susie's paper bag.

"Oh, you beast!" cried Susie. "You've ruined
all my work!" She picked up the can of red paint
and poured it over Alfred's bag.

That did it. They started to quarrel and fight
and the paint went flying in all directions.

Susie sulked. "I want to go home," she said.
Alfred sulked and said, "I wish you'd never
come in the first place!"

"You're horrid!" exclaimed Susie, stalking off with
her half-finished, messed-up costume.
"Anyway," snorted Alfred, "I can do much better on my own!"

Back at her home Susie got out her sewing box and the rag bag. "I'll show that Alfred," she muttered, starting to snip and cut furiously.

Later in the day Alfred's mother brought something
to eat. "Where's Susie?" she asked.
"I don't know and I don't care!" Alfred replied.

Next door Susie's mother was surprised. "I thought
you were at Alfred's house," she said.
"I don't like Alfred anymore," said Susie. "I'm
making my costume alone."

Night came and everything was quiet.
Susie's front door opened. A terrible monster appeared.

At the same time Alfred's front door opened.
Out stepped a second terrible monster.

The monsters met under the street lamp.
"HELP! HELP!" squeaked one of them.

"SOMEONE SAVE ME!" squealed the other.

"Ooh! Aah! EEEEK!" they shrieked wildly.

Suddenly they recognized each other's voices and
stopped and turned.

"Is that really you, Susie? You look fantastic!"

"And you look amazing, Alfred! Let's go
to the party together!"

So they set off.

On the way they were joined by all sorts of weird friends.

At the Halloween party they had games, lots of
lovely food, and dancing. There was a competition
for the best costume.

Alfred and Susie won first prize together as Mr.
and Mrs. Monster. Their friend Sam came in second.
Nobody knew the little person who came in third.
He must have come from the other side of town.

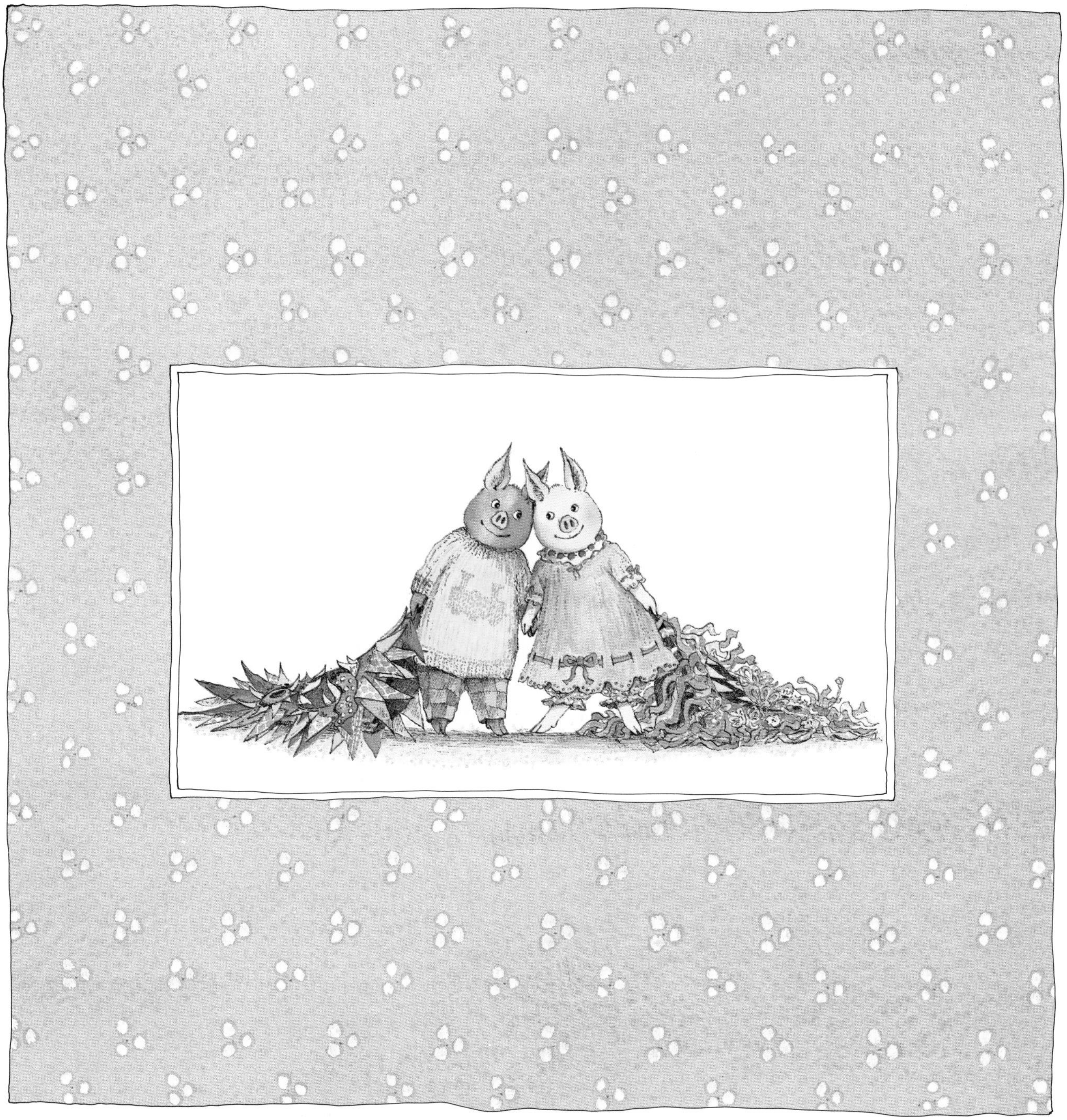